"Joey Rockaway and his enterprising friend Jack McGurk are intrigued with new-boy-in-town Willie Sandowsky for two reasons: He has a remarkably keen sense of smell, and he has a mystery to solve—the disappearence of his brand-new catcher's mitt. How the McGurk Organization ('Private investigations, mysteries solved') sniffs out the subject and recovers the missing mitt is disclosed in a funny, first-person narrative, which moves briskly yet manages to include all the practical, homely details necessary for credibility and humor."                                    —*The Horn Book*

**BY THE SAME AUTHOR**

*My Kid Sister*
*Here Comes Parren*
*The Dragon That Lived Under Manhattan*

FOR OLDER READERS:
*The Doughnut Dropout*
*Manhattan Is Missing*
*Louie's Lot*
*Louie's S.O.S.*
*Top Boy at Twisters Creek*
*The Secret Winners*

# The Nose Knows

# The Nose Knows

## A McGurk Mystery

### E. W. Hildick

Illustrated by Unada Gliewe

**tempo books**

GROSSET & DUNLAP, INC.

Publishers    New York

*To William Popham McDougal*

# CONTENTS

# The Nose Knows

# CHAPTER ONE

# *The Nose*

"Hey! Take a look at him! What's he doing?"

McGurk was pointing past some bushes when he said this. He was pointing past the bushes into the back yard next to ours.

"That's the new kid," I said. "His folks have come to live here. They moved in this morning. They call him—"

"I'm not asking what he's called. And I'm not asking what he did this morning. I'm asking what he's doing right *now!*"

McGurk was whispering. He was whispering in that raspy way he has when he is all excited or curious. And, sure enough, the new kid was acting strange.

Very strange indeed.

But first let me tell you who's who.

I am Joey Rockaway. I am 10 years, 2 months, 3 weeks, and 4 days old. I like to get things exactly right. That's why it is my job to tell you all about what happened.

McGurk is my best friend. His given name is Jack, but only his mother and father and other relatives use it. We all call him McGurk. He likes that, except when we fight and call him McGurk the Jerk. Then he gets mad.

McGurk is 10 also. The months and weeks and things don't matter with him. He's not the kind of guy to stop and count. He's not the kind of guy to stop and *anything*.

In fact, right now it was a wonder he was

2

stopping on our side of the bushes, he was so curious.

He kept standing first on one leg then the other. Leaning forward. Screwing his eyes up. Peering. And as he stood and leaned and peered like this, he crunched away at some candy. "Crunch, swock, click . . . Crunch, swock, click," he was going. Destroying these hard fruity candies one after another, like they were peanuts, and not offering me a single one.

McGurk almost never offers anyone any of his candies. It's not that he's greedy. He'll give you one if you ask him. It's just that he never stops to think about it.

Anyway, more details about him and me later. (Things like his red hair and my brown hair, and him with a top tooth missing on the left and me wearing glasses.) Right now I have to tell you what was happening to make us so curious. Because—as I said before—this new kid certainly was acting very strange.

There was a pile of boxes in their yard that afternoon. Big ones, little ones, medium ones.

Some were made of cardboard, some of wood.
They were all empty. We knew this on account
of the way he was tossing them around.

"They must have been what they packed
their things in," I whispered.

"Eh?" grunted McGurk, still peering and
chewing.

"The boxes. They must have used them for
packing. They—"

"Yeah, yeah! I can see that. But what's he
*doing?* He—he looks like he's *trying them on!*"

And this was true enough.

With the small and medium boxes he'd do it
standing up. I mean he would stick a box over
his head, and turn from side to side, and maybe
bow a little, and sometimes go right up on
tippy-toe, and then he'd groan. Yes, groan. All
hollow and echoey, inside the box. I tell you, it
was kind of spooky the way he did this, like
something out of a Creature Feature. Like the
Man Without A Head. Or the Thing In The
Iron Mask.

Even Sammy, the Henshaws' beagle, wasn't

for getting too close. Usually that dog likes to be into anything strange that goes on. But this time—no. Out from behind a bush on the opposite side from us he trotted. Then stopped dead. Staring. Nose twitching. One front paw up off the ground. You could tell that the sight of a box with arms and legs had him all curious. But then:

"Yee-ergh!" groaned the box.

And that was enough for Sammy.

Off he flew, ears flat, tail down, as if he'd seen a ghost that was out to get him. The ghost of a mailman, maybe.

Anyway, after every time the new kid groaned like this, he would bend down to the pile again, whip off the box that was on his head and whip on another—quick as that— before we'd time to see his face.

"I think you have a cuckoo come to live next to you," said McGurk, after a while. "I do really. And if he tries to put this *next* box on his head, I'll be sure of it."

I could see what McGurk meant. The next

5

box was a really big one. One of those big square wood ones you could curl up and hide in. If the new kid tried to wear that for a hat it would slip right down over his shoulders and pin him down for keeps. Unless of course we rescued him.

Well, that guy tried.

After groaning and throwing off the last cardboard box, he bent down and tried to lift the big wooden one.

Then he changed his mind.

"Look at him *now!*" gasped McGurk.

For, with a groan that was half a growl, the new kid dove into that box. Just dove in there, head first, so that all we could see of him for around a minute were his blue jeans waving about in the air, and his red socks, and his sneakers.

Then slowly the long, skinny legs stopped waving, and they kind of drooped, and his feet went back on the ground, and out of the box came the rest of him, and at last we got a good look at his face.

Thin.

Pale.

And sad. Very very sad.

Also it had one of the biggest, longest noses I ever saw on a kid.

It was the sort of nose that makes a face look sad even when its owner is happy.

"Maybe he's been trying to hide it from us," whispered McGurk, thinking exactly what I was thinking.

But the new kid hadn't even spotted us yet.

He was bending over the boxes again. This time, though, he wasn't aiming to try them on. No. He was sniffing at them, very gently, very carefully, around the edges. And it wasn't until he'd put his nose to work on a medium-size container labeled JAFFA ORANGES that he saw us.

His big dark eyes went bigger, over the edge of the box, and he still kept on with his sniffing. But he said, "Hi!"—so we decided to come out from behind the bushes and join him.

"Hi!" said McGurk, stepping up to the edge

of the scattered pile of boxes. "I'm McGurk and this here's Joey Rockaway." He was speaking very gently and kindly, still thinking the new kid was some kind of nut. "Who are you?"

The new kid sighed and tossed the box away from his nose.

"Me?" he said, managing a wobbly kind of a smile but still looking very sad. "I'm Willie Sandowsky. We just moved in here. All the way from Cleveland. That's in Ohio, up near Lake—"

"Sure, sure!" said McGurk. "Save the geography for Joey here. What *I'm* curious about is these boxes. What's with them that makes you so sad?"

Now I am used to McGurk getting straight to the point and cutting out all the chitchat. Strangers aren't. They usually look startled and back off some.

Willie didn't.

He might have known McGurk all his life, the way he simply shrugged and said:

"It is what's *not* with these boxes makes me sad."

8

"Oh, and what is that, Willie?" asked McGurk, taking out the last of his candies.

"My brand new catcher's mitt," said Willie. "A present from my Aunt Mabel."

And he looked so sad just then that McGurk took pity on him and offered him the candy without being asked.

"No, thanks," said Willie. "It'll spoil my sense of smell."

"Catcher's mitt?" I said.

"Smell?" said McGurk.

"Yeah," said Willie. "Everything's been unpacked and I can't find that mitt anyplace. Now I'm sniffing around to see if Mom packed it after all. She says she's sure she did, but it's beginning to look like she's wrong again. . . . I mean it's beginning to *smell* like she's wrong," he added, picking up another box and sniffing gently.

"Ha!" laughed McGurk, winking at me. "Looks like you have a *joker* for a neighbor, Joey. Willie's been putting us on."

"I wish I *was* only kidding," grunted Willie. "I sure do."

"Come *on*!" said McGurk. "You're not trying to tell us you can *smell* whether a catcher's mitt has been packed or not?"

"Well, I can so!" said Willie. "I was born with a very sensitive nose. I can tell you nearly everything that was packed in these boxes."

"Betcha can't!" said McGurk.

"Betcha I can!" said Willie.

"Go on, then," said McGurk.

Then Willie gave us a demonstration I will never forget.

# CHAPTER TWO

## *Willie Proves His Point*

"First," said Willie, picking up one of the medium-size boxes, "what would you say had been packed in here?"

"Easy!" said McGurk. "Prunes."

"Eh?" said Willie.

"It says it on the side," said McGurk.

He was pointing to the label:

*Calfrute Prunes*

IN 12 OUNCE (340 GM.) PACKS

"Nargh!" said Willie. "I don't mean what it had inside originally. I mean what Mom packed inside it to bring from Cleveland."

McGurk shrugged.

"Sniff!" said Willie, shoving the box under his nose. "And tell me what you smell."

McGurk sniffed and shrugged again.

"Just a kind of papery smell is all."

"That's because you don't have a sensitive nose," said Willie. "You take a sniff, Joey. Yours looks more sensitive."

But even though I sniffed more carefully than McGurk, all I could catch was a whiff of orange candy from McGurk's breath.

"Well, I'll tell you," said Willie, sniffing at it himself. "In this box Mom must have packed things from the bathroom. I get a distinct aroma of hair-spray. Also traces of foot powder. The toothpaste smell is very strong—I'm surprised even your noses couldn't pick that up. And right down in the corner there is a pocket of iodine."

"No kidding?" murmured McGurk. He looked very impressed. "Tell us about some of the others."

And Willie did just that.

Now me, I wasn't sure. I mean I didn't think Willie was kidding on purpose. He looked too serious and still very sad. No. But I did wonder if he wasn't kidding *himself*. You know. Simply imagining the smells.

For example. In a cardboard box with this label:

**KAUFMAN'S
KAT
CHOW**

72 LARGE CANS

he said his mother had packed some vegetables which they'd grown themselves back home in Cleveland.

"Mostly spinach," he said. "But also some mint."

And in a box with this printed on the side:

> STORE IN A COOL PLACE
> TO RIPEN, REMOVE WRAPPINGS
> AND HOLD AT ROOM TEMPERATURE

he swore that his nose could pick up faint traces of the original contents.

"Apples," he said. "Yeah. Definitely apples. But what Mom packed in it for the move was winter socks, sweaters, things like that. I can smell the wool from here. Slightly prickly and a bit oily."

McGurk was looking excited.

"Willie," he said, "you're a genius! Or your *nose* is a genius. Right, Joey?"

"Maybe it is," said Willie, making a long sad sniff go running up it. "But it can't smell out what isn't there. And now I'm *sure* Mom missed out on packing that mitt."

"Forget about it!" said McGurk, clipping him on the shoulder. "With a nose like that, you shouldn't have a thing to worry about, Willie."

He was grinning all over his face.

"Huh?" Willie looked at me. It was now *his* turn to wonder who was the nut in our neighborhood. I just shrugged, while McGurk went on:

"No! With a nose like that we can solve all sorts of mysteries. We can do what I've always wanted to do. We can start a detective bureau.

The McGurk Organization. Investigations Made. Mysteries Solved." He said it as if it was another label he was reading. "We can use our basement as an office."

Willie was frowning. He kicked moodily at a box marked FRAGILE and said:

"What has my nose got to do with it?"

"Why, don't you see? It'll be like having a bloodhound. But a bloodhound that can talk!"

"Hey, now hold it!" said Willie. He sounded a bit miffed. "If—" Then he stopped and frowned, thinking some more, and when he was through with that his face brightened. "Gee!" he said. "I'd never have thought of that!"

Me, I had my doubts. There's a big difference between a dog that can really smell faint traces of this and that and a kid who only *thinks* he can. But there was no stopping McGurk.

"You've heard of Private Eyes," he said. "Well, you'll be the nation's first Private Nose, Willie."

"Gee!" was all Willie could say by now.

"Yeah," I said softly, trying to put the brakes on McGurk, "and McGurk will be the nation's first Private Mouth."

"I heard that!" he said. "Now think of something smart for yourself. Like the Private Heel."

"Nuh-huh," I said, winking at Willie. "I've already thought of something for me. The Private *Brain*."

But I should have known better than to try and outsmart McGurk when he's in that mood.

"All right, wise guy," he said. "Just for that, you can be the one who keeps all the records. You can write down all the case notes with that typewriter of yours."

Well, I guess it's a good thing at that. I mean knowing how to operate a typewriter and having a good, tidy mind. Otherwise I'd never keep on top of the job, all the cases McGurk keeps finding for us.

But I've not really begun telling you about our very first one yet.

"O.K.?" said McGurk, that afternoon in Willie's back yard, among the empty boxes.

"You're both with me in this?"

"Why, sure!" said Willie, looking cheerful for the very first time.

"Sure, why not?" I said.

"Right," said McGurk, already on the move, heading for his house. "Let's go. We have to get our office organized."

But Willie's smile had gone again. He stood right where he was and shook his head.

"Sorry, fellers," he said. "I have to get back to my search."

"For *what?*" said McGurk, looking annoyed. (He hates to be held up when he's got a great idea burning away in his brain.) "For some old *catcher's mitt?*"

"I told you," said Willie. "It was brand new."

"So all right!" said McGurk, still impatient. "For some old *brand-new* catcher's mitt, then. Forget it. It'll turn up."

"Yeah, but what if it doesn't?" said Willie.

"Well, get your aunt to buy you another," said McGurk. "That's soon taken care of. . . . Now come on. We're wasting time."

But still Willie hung back.

"You don't know my aunt," he said. "She's coming to visit us next weekend. If she doesn't see me with that mitt, enjoying it, she'll never give me anything ever again.... She's very generous, too," he said, extra mournful now. "When she sees her gifts being enjoyed. But if you lose any of them...pow! That's *it*. That's the last thing *she'll* ever give you."

This time McGurk didn't have a quick answer, so I got a chance to speak.

"She sounds pretty mean, if you ask me," I said.

"Nobody did ask you!" said Willie, suddenly fierce. "I tell you it's just the way she is. If you don't lose or louse up her presents she's the generousest—"

"The most generous," I said, trying to put him right.

"Yeah," said Willie. "That's what I just said. The generousest aunt a guy could wish for. Why," he said, "she's only got to hear I've found a new hobby or interest and—*click!*—she opens her purse and says, 'Here's a ten-dollar bill, Willie. Go buy yourself the right equipment.' "

"Is that *so?*" murmured McGurk, getting all gleamy-eyed again. "*Any* new hobby or interest?"

"Sure," said Willie. "Like stamp-collecting one time. Or like—"

"Detecting? Being a detective?"

"Sure," said Willie. "That too, I guess."

McGurk patted him on the shoulder.

"Your worries are over, Willie," he said. "Soon as we get the office fixed up, we'll make that mitt our first case. We'll give you all the help you need. Now come on. The office, the office. Let's go to it."

# CHAPTER THREE

## *The Office*

BEING MCGURK'S BEST friend is the hardest work I know. No kidding. Sometimes, after a vacation, I feel glad to get back to school. I mean for the rest.

When McGurk said we'd use his basement room, I thought:

"Oh-oh! Here we go again!"

Willie didn't think that, you could tell.

## The Office

But Willie didn't know McGurk. Or his basement room. And I did.

So what does McGurk's basement room have to do with hard work?

Listen.

If you had seen it at one time, you would have thought it was just another little store-room, between the game room and the boiler room.

But that was before Mr. McGurk let him have it for a den. That was before Mr. McGurk said:

"No more using your bedroom for a den. I am tired of watching the living-room ceiling bounce up and down. I am tired of watching bits of plaster shake loose. I am tired of wondering if I am living under a poolroom."

So McGurk got the basement room for a den. Then there were only maybe a few mice and a ground hog or two to wonder what was happening above them. Then Mr. and Mrs. McGurk could relax in peace. Then the hard work started for anyone fool enough to be McGurk's best friend.

You see, he kept changing his mind about that room. To most kids a den is just a den. But McGurk, no. He has to keep changing it into other things. And since McGurk has had that basement room, you know what he's made it into, different times? He's made it into these:

A Pirates' Lair;

A Western Saloon;

A Space Ship (with one corner acting as Mission Control);

A Clearing in Sherwood Forest;

A Bank (for staging hold-ups);

A Hospital Room (with an Operating Table in the corner);

A Polaris Submarine;

Doctor Frankenstein McGurk's Secret Laboratory; and

The Office of the Junior President of the U.S.A. (That was the time when he thought there should be a separate President for kids under 12.)

*Now* do you see where the hard work comes in?

Clearing that room of the last bunch of junk ready for the next. That is where the hard work comes in. Like getting rid of all those bottles we collected for the Dodge City saloon. Like dragging that heavy old table from one corner to another, and scraping all the red paint off it that we'd used for blood the time we operated on Sue Gallo's Teddy bear for a fracture of the squeaker. Like trying to get rid of the old iron fire screen we'd used for the bank teller's grill. Like sweeping up the mess of dead leaves from the branches we'd brought in for Robin Hood's secret camp....

Well, this particular afternoon was no different. I won't go into details about how we cleared away all the pipes, and old lawn-mower parts, and old coffee percolators, and all the millions of things that had gone into the Frankenstein laboratory. No. All I'll say is that by the time we'd gotten the room clear for the detective office stuff, Willie was looking bushed. His face looked sadder and his nose looked even longer and I could tell he was wishing he'd stayed home and helped with the unpacking there.

But McGurk was only just warming up.

"I want the table in the center," he said. "Stretched right across the room. Then it won't be easy for suspects to make a break for it, when we're questioning them behind it."

So we dragged the old table into its new position.

"Chairs are easy," he said. "You and Willie can have these two. Me, I'll use the old rocker from up in the attic. It's the nearest to a big swivel chair I know, and I should have brought it down for my President chair. Well, now I've just got to have it. Come on."

That was one *very* heavy chair, believe me.

"Next," said McGurk, even before Willie and I had recovered, "we need files. Places to put our records and things. Cabinets, like in offices."

For one horrible minute I thought he knew another corner of the attic upstairs where there were some of those heavy steel cabinets he was talking about. Then:

"I know," he said, snapping his fingers. "Some of those boxes in your back yard, Willie. Let's go."

That wasn't too bad. They were light enough, those boxes. And anyway, he only wanted three.

"This one," he said, when we'd taken them back to the basement, "will be just right for the records of all the mysteries we're gonna solve."

It sure was big enough. It was the prune box.

"Great!" said Willie, beginning to cheer up a bit.

"I guess," I said, not so cheerful. (I mean, I was the one who was going to have to type all those records.)

"O.K., then," said McGurk.

Then he scrawled over the words CALFRUTE PRUNES with a big black marking pen and wrote in the new label. Now it said:

MYSTERIES SOLVED
IN 12-OUNCE (340 GM.) PACKS

"Hey!" said Willie, starting to grin, "shouldn't you—"

But there was no stopping McGurk. I could have told him that.

"And this one," he was saying, picking up the cat food box, "can be for the mystery we happen to be working on at the moment."

"That's even bigger," I said. "Shouldn't we use that for all the solved mysteries?"

He shook his head.

"No. Because this won't be just for records. We'll make a special compartment in it for any clues we find."

And he scrawled over the cat's face and the words KAUFMAN'S KAT CHOW, and again he didn't bother about the small print. So this time when he'd finished the label said:


LATEST MYSTERY
RECORDS AND CLUES
72 LARGE CANS


Then he picked up the last—the apple box.

"Don't tell me," said Willie. "This is gonna be for *unsolved* mysteries. . . . No?"

McGurk was looking as if he was going to

fire Willie before that kid had even started
being a detective.

"*Un*solved mysteries? What kind of talk is
that? When the McGurk Organization gets going there will *be* no unsolved mysteries, fella."

And he was so fierce he didn't bother to
scrawl anything out. He simply scrawled the
new label *in*, so it now read:

DETAILS OF SUSPECTS

STORE IN A COOL PLACE

TO RIPEN, REMOVE WRAPPINGS

AND HOLD AT ROOM TEMPERATURE.

After that, both Willie and McGurk took it a
bit easier.

Not me, though.

Oh, no!

McGurk had found some thin sheets of cardboard in the bottom of the apple—sorry!—I
mean the *suspects* box.

"Just the thing," he said.

"For what?" I said.

"For I.D. cards," he said.

"What's I.D. cards?" said Willie.

"Indentification cards," said McGurk. "All detectives have them. . . . Think these will fit in your typewriter, Joey?"

"Sure," I said. "But—"

"Good! Go get it. Oh, and bring an old snapshot of yourself at the same time. Any one will do, so long as it's fairly recent. You too, Willie. Go dig out a snapshot of *yourself*. I'll be getting the scissors."

By the time we'd gotten back, McGurk had already roughed out in pencil the way he wanted the cards to look.

"O.K.," he said. "Start typing."

And here's how our three I.D. cards came out—after I'd typed them, and we'd stuck in the pictures we'd cut from our snapshots, and we'd spit on our fingers and rubbed them in the dirt on the floor to make the fingerprints:

Officer's Name:
    Jack P. McGurk
Age: 10 years
Height:  4ft. 1o ins.
Weight:
Hair color: Red
      Eyes color: Green
Birthmarks etc.:  Freckles

FINGERPRINTS  L/H     FINGERPRINTS R/H

Officer's Name:
    Joseph B. Rockaway
Age:  10 yrs, 2xmonths
Height: 4ft 10½ins  Weight:
Hair color:  Brown (medium)
Eyes: Blue
Birthmarks: Mole shaped like
kite, 3ins above left knee.

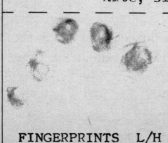

FINGERPRINTS  L/H     FINGERPRINTS  R/H

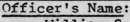

Officer's Name:
        William S. Sandowsky
Age: 9yrs (nearly 10)
Height: 5ft 0ins
Weight:
Hair color: Dark Brown
Eyes: Brown
Birthmarks:  None

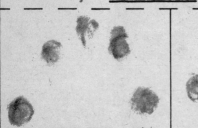

FINGERPRINTS   L/H          FINGERPRINTS   R/H

The dotted line along the center is where the cards were folded. On the outside at the front they looked like this:

I.D. CARD

Officer

*Rockaway*

THE McGurk
ORGANIZATION

INVESTIGATIONS

On the outside at the back:

```
This card
is the
property
of the
McGURK
ORGANIZATION



Not to be
loaned,
borrowed,
rented,
sold,
bought,
or copied.
Or else.
```

The weights we left out, you will notice. McGurk was in too much of a hurry to let us go use the bathroom scales, and I guess we still haven't gotten around to filling out that part. Myself, I would have done this long ago, being very exact and all. But then, how exact can you *be* about weights, which keep changing so much? Even heights, really. And that is also why I crossed out the months and weeks I had started to add after my age.

While I was typing the cards, McGurk asked if I could also supply paper for the records. I was going to say there wasn't much chance, but I didn't have to.

"My father is a paper *salesman*," said Willie. "He's got stacks and stacks of samples. He lets me use as much as I want."

"What are you waiting for, then?" said McGurk. "Go get some, why don't you?"

So Willie went for the paper and I finished off the cards. But even when they were all ready, Willie still hadn't returned.

"I wonder what's keeping him," I said.

"He'll be back," said McGurk. "Just give me a hand with this."

This was a notice he was printing on some spare card. He wasn't sure of some of the spelling, so he hadn't inked it in yet. It was the big notice for the door and he wanted to get it right. So I helped him with that and very nice it looked, too, as we pinned it up.

"Beautiful!" said McGurk, standing back to admire it and nearly falling into the boiler.

"Not bad,," I said. "Hello, here's Willie back at last."

"*Now* all we need," said McGurk, not even turning his head from the notice, "is our first case."

Then Willie spoke.

"I thought we'd decided on that already," he said, and his face was glummer than ever. "The Mystery of the Missing Mitt."

"Oh, *that!*" said McGurk. "Well, yes. But that's no mystery really. That's just something your mother forgot to pack."

"Nuh-huh!" said Willie. "She didn't forget. She packed it all right. It vanished *after* reaching here." He held out the pack of paper he'd brought along. "Here. Just smell *this!*"

# CHAPTER FOUR

# *McGurk Investigates*

THERE WAS REALLY no need for Willie to hold out the pack.

That pack of paper *reeked*. It reeked of something that was:

tangy (though not like lemons, tangy);
sharp (it could cut through any other smell);

prickly (it was bad enough to make your
  eyes water);
stinging (it did things to the inside of
  your nose); and
leathery — very leathery — but not *real*
  leathery.

I knew that smell. It is what they use on
imitation leather to make it smell like real
leather. Some kind of chemical. And I knew it
so well because only last Christmas my father
had had to bury a pair of driving gloves that
had been given an overdose of the stuff. Great-
Aunt Lucy from Minnesota had sent him the
gloves for Christmas and they'd smelled so
strong they made the turkey taste of leather. No
kidding. I even think it was the smell of them
that caused one of my goldfish to die, two days
later. Anyway, Dad ended up by burying them
at the bottom of the yard. He said at least the
underground smell might stop the Henshaws'
dog Sammy from burying his bones there,
though I can't say it was strong enough for
that.

"*Pow!*" said McGurk, when he took a deep sniff at Willie's pack of paper. "Does all your old man's paper smell like this?"

"It's not the paper," said Willie. "It's what was packed along with the paper. It's the smell of my brand-new catcher's mitt."

Once again I got to wondering about Willie's nose. I mean it didn't take any *special* nose to smell *that*.

McGurk wiped his eyes.

"You mean that mitt did arrive here after all?"

Willie was looking a bit sore.

"That's what I keep telling ya!" he said.

"Well, then," said McGurk, "if it's in the house it should be easy to track down. If that's only the smell it leaves *around*," he added, wiping his eyes again and backing off.

"That's just *it!*" said Willie. "Apart from the crate that has the paper in it, and the paper itself, there's not a whiff of it in the whole house."

"So?" said McGurk, still keeping his distance.

"So it's obvious," said Willie. "Somebody must have snuck off with it since this morning."

"Unless it snuck off by itself," I said.

"How's that?" said McGurk.

He was sitting on the rocking chair now, rocking thoughtfully.

"Anything reeking as bad as that might just be able to do its own walking," I said.

"This is no time for jokes!" said McGurk, standing up and leaving the chair rocking like mad. "We have to investigate this while the scent's still hot."

"Some *scent!*" I said. "Anyway, why all the sweat?"

"My aunt arrives in four days is why," said Willie.

"Right!" said McGurk. "And Willie's got a new hobby. We could use one of those ten-dollar bills for fingerprint powder and magnifying glasses—one for each of us—and—and—"

"So what?" I said. "Even if we don't find the mitt, we can always put in a substitute. I have one you can borrow, Willie. It's not brand new, but it's not so old either. And you can always say you've been using it so much that—no?"

"Nuh-huh!" said Willie. "No chance. You see she likes to do what she calls *personalize* her presents. And this one, she wrote on the leather with that black ink that doesn't rub off: 'Happy Catching!' And signed it." He groaned deeply. "'Your loving Aunt Mabel.' In her own handwriting."

I withdrew my offer at once. I mean, loaning a guy your mitt is one thing. Having to write *that* stuff on it—in indelible ink—is something else again. Even if it fooled this Aunt Mabel—which didn't sound likely.

The other two must have been thinking the same. They were already on their way to question the Sandowskys.

Both Mr. And Mrs. Sandowsky had been very busy. So I guess it is A+ to them for being so patient with us. I mean it's not many grownups who are able to smile at the end of a busy house-moving day when three kids burst in on them, flashing I.D. cards.

"Gee!" said Mr. Sandowsky. "I hope you don't suspect *me* of this!"

He is a big guy, with yellow hair and a little snubby nose and laughing eyes. Not a bit like Willie.

"That depends, sir," said McGurk. "*My* father once snuck off with a toy trumpet of mine. . . ."

"I can give my husband an alibi," said Mrs. Sandowsky. "He's been with me all day. And why should he want to steal his own son's catcher's mit? A trumpet I can understand. But why a catcher's mitt?"

She also wasn't much like Willie. Fair hair, quite plump, round smiling face, ordinary nose.

"I'll ask the questions, ma'am," said McGurk. "Thank you. . . . My assistant Rockaway here will record the answers in his notebook. Willie, you just have another sniff around the house to make absolutely sure."

But neither McGurk's questions, nor my writing down the answers, nor Willie's sniffing around again, made any difference. Except that the mystery got deeper.

Mr. and Mrs. Sandowsky were ruled out. So were the moving men.

"The crate was all nailed up," said Mr. Sandowsky. "I didn't take the lid off until after the men had gone."

"Ah!" said McGurk. "So you actually *saw* the mitt as well as smelled it, did you?"

"Well—uh—no."

McGurk frowned. He looked hard at Mr. Sandowsky. Then he turned to Mrs. Sandowsky.

"But, ma'am, *you* said you remember putting the mitt right at the top. Here—"

He took my notebook and pointed to where I'd written one of Mrs. Sandowsky's answers:

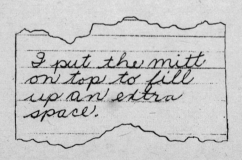

*I put the mitt on top to fill up an extra space.*

"Yes, yes," said Mr. Sandowsky. "I know she said that. But what I'm saying is that I didn't look inside the crate. Just as I was taking the lid off, the doorbell rang and Willie's mother here shouted up to say we had visitors."

"Up?" I said.

"Yeah. The crate was in the room upstairs that I plan on using as a den."

"Get that down," said McGurk to me.

Then to Mr. Sandowsky he said:

"Visitors, sir?"

"Oh, *yes!*" said Mrs. Sandowsky. "I remember. The Welcome Wagon came. Your mother. And yours, Joey. And some of the other ladies. And some children."

"*Aha!*" said McGurk, looking very alert.

"That's important?" said Mr. Sandowsky.

"Yes, *sir!*" said McGurk. "Because I'd just gotten around to thinking. Since it wasn't either of you, or the moving men, it must have been an outside job. Somebody from around here must have snuck in and taken that mitt."

"Oh, gosh!" said Mr. Sandowsky, beginning to look as sad as Willie. "And there was I, thinking we'd moved into a low-crime neighborhood."

"But who would *do* a thing like that?" said Mrs. Sandowsky. "A *sneak thief?* From around *here?*"

"I'm not saying it's any ordinary sneak thief," said McGurk. "I think we're up against a special type." He turned and looked grimly at me and Willie. "You paying attention, men? We're up against some kind of nut. A Catcher's Mitt Nut. Some poor nut who happened to come in, see it—maybe just sniff it—and couldn't resist it."

The way he said this made me shiver down my back. The others were looking a bit uneasy also.

Then McGurk snapped his fingers at me and turned back to Mr. and Mrs. Sandowsky.

"I want a list of all these Welcome Wagon people. The ones who came here right after the moving men had left."

# CHAPTER FIVE

## *The New Member*

HERE IS THE list of all the people who came with the Welcome Wagon, just as I wrote it down:

Mrs. McGurk
Mrs. Rockaway
Mrs. Henshaw
Mrs. Lorrimore
Mrs. Gallo
Mrs. Grieg
     Wanda Grieg
     Sue Gallo
     Tony Gallo

The three on the right are just the kids who tagged along. Wanda is 9, Sue is 5, and Tony 3. O.K.

So what was the next step?

"Willie," said McGurk, "if any of them's been handling that mitt, will their hands still smell of it?"

"What do *you* think?" I said, remembering those driving gloves, and the turkey, and the goldfish.

"I'm asking Willie," said McGurk.

"Sure," said Willie.

"Right," said McGurk. "So the problem is this. How to get to smell all their hands without them suspecting?"

"Quite a problem," said Mr. Sandowsky. "Considering it's getting so late and it's time Willie was washing up ready for supper."

"Gee, yes!" I said, looking at the clock. "I should have been home half an hour ago myself."

"No sweat," said McGurk. "Whoever took that mitt will probably handle it again tomorrow. And by then I'll probably have figured out a way of getting a sniff at their hands. . . . Thanks for your cooperation, Mrs. Sandowsky, Mr. Sandowsky. See Willie gets a good night's sleep. We'll be needing his nose nice and fresh tomorrow."

Well, it was a problem sure enough, but not with our two mothers, of course. I mean if a guy can't get to smell his mother's hand without her suspecting anything, that guy isn't *fit* to be a detective.

The way McGurk did it was like this.

He told his mother he liked the smell of her new hand cream. When she said, "What hand cream?" he said, "The stuff you've rubbed on your hands." And when she said she hadn't rubbed any stuff on her hands, he said:

"C'm here, let me smell. *Mff! mff!* Gee, it must be just the soap!"

The way I did it was different. Slicker, also.

I said, "Mom, how did you get that splinter in the back of your middle finger?"

"What splinter?"

I said, "C'm here, let me show you." Then I put my eye closer, which meant putting my nose closer, and I said:

"Gosh, I must have made a mistake!"

Anyway, the result in both cases was the same. McGurk's mother and mine were in the clear. We crossed them off the list.

The next day, we started nice and early. The kids on the list looked like being even easier than our two mothers. To little Sue and little Tony, McGurk simply said:

"Hey, hold your hands out and let Willie here smell them."

And those two little kids did it, just like that, and Willie said he smelled tomato sauce quite strong but nothing else. So they were in the clear.

But with Wanda Grieg it was tough.

*Very* tough.

Wanda is a girl. She has long brown hair and she wears dull old jeans with bright new cloth flowers stitched on them. She is *quite* a girl, too. She—but you'll soon see what I mean.

For instance. That morning. When we caught up with her. Know what she was doing?

She was just getting down from the tall tree in front of her house. She can climb that tree quicker than some boys I can mention, and she is always using different ways to the top.

But did McGurk stop to think about all this?

Did he stop to think how he'd have to handle a girl like that in a special way?

No, sir. He did not.

"Wanda," he said, straight out, just like with the little kids, "hold your hands out."

Wanda lifted one hand, sure. But only to brush her hair out of her eyes with.

"Why?"

Because Willie here wants to smell them."

She gave Willie a glance that made him blush to the tip of that nose.

"What's he want to smell my hands for?"

"That's *our* business," said McGurk.

"Yeah," said Wanda. "And these are *my* hands."

McGurk seemed to brighten up at this. He turned to us.

"Looks like we're onto something, men."
Wanda frowned.

"Onto something? What d'you mean?"

"I mean it looks like you might have something to hide," said McGurk, making his eyes go all narrow.

"I've got nothing to hide," said Wanda. "Look for yourself."

She held out both hands, palms up. But when Willie went toward her with his nose twitching, she folded up her right hand into a fist and he backed off quick.

"Is this some kind of dumb joke, McGurk?" she said then.

"It is not," said McGurk. "It is a very serious case we are investigating."

That made her eyes go wide. She brushed back the hair again to give those eyes a better chance to see McGurk's face.

"Case? Investigating? Oh, boy! Is this a *mystery*, then?"

"It is," said McGurk.

"Hey! I'm good at mysteries," she said. "Will you let me help?"

"Yes," said McGurk. "By letting us smell your hands."

She backed off, fists tight again and behind her back.

"Nuh-huh! Tell me first why it's so important."

Well, I suppose we could have rushed her. But it probably would have meant climbing up that tree after her. And maybe getting kicked in the nose on the way up so we couldn't smell anything when we did get her.

So we told her, and her eyes went wider still.

"Golly!" she said.

"O.K.," said McGurk. "Now the hands."

But she still wasn't ready to cooperate.

"Not unless you let me join your organization," she said.

"No way!" said McGurk, very firm.

"But that's dumb!" she said. "You *need* a woman on the team. There's all sorts of things women detectives can do that men can't."

McGurk sneered. He's great on sneering. He can make his top lip go snaking up to his left eye until it nearly touches it.

"Like *what?*" he said. "What things?"

"Like figuring out ways of getting to smell ladies' hands without getting them all suspicious the way you got me. I mean, you still have four more lady suspects to investigate after me."

"Well. . . ." said McGurk slowly, the sneer wiped off his face.

But she wasn't through yet.

"And one of those four is my mother. And she's gone back to bed with one of her bad headaches and won't be getting up again today. How're you gonna get to sniff *her* hand without me? Just tell me *that!*"

McGurk shrugged.

"Maybe we won't need to investigate any further after you," he said, his eyes all narrow again.

But there's no stopping Wanda either, when *she* gets going.

"And already I've thought of a brilliant idea to get Mrs. Gallo and Mrs. Lorrimore and Mrs.

Henshaw to let you smell *their* hands."

"What idea?" said McGurk, looking interested.

"If I tell you, will you let me join?"

McGurk thought awhile.

"O.K.," he said. "If it's good enough."

"All right then," said Wanda. "This is my
idea."

She looked at Willie and me a bit scornfully,
then started whispering in McGurk's ear.

At first he frowned.

Then he twitched the side of his face she
was whispering into, and the frown was shaken
out of it.

Then he laughed out loud.

"Hey, that's a *great* idea!" he said.

"I can join then?"

"It's a deal," he said. "But only if you're clear
yourself. Hold out your hands."

This time she did, and we all sniffed and
McGurk was satisfied (and I'll say this for him:
he always keeps his word).

"Joey," he said, "make out an I.D. card for

Wanda, soon as we're through checking out these other hands."

Well, I did, and here's how Wanda's card looked:

**Officer's Name:** Wanda Grieg
**Age:** 9 years
**Height:** 4ft. 6ins.(without
            heels)        **Weight:**
**Hair Color:** ash-blonde,
            with honey highlights.
**Eyes:** a beautiful greeny-gray
            with golden flecks.
**Birthmarks:** beauty spot on left shoulder

FINGERPRINTS  L/H        FINGERPRINTS  R/H

Some of those descriptions she insisted on dictating herself.

The prints she made with some of her mother's eyeshadow, not spit and dirt.

But anyway, making her card out came after we'd put this great idea of hers into operation. So next I will tell you what it was and how it worked.

# CHAPTER SIX

# *Wanda's Plan*

THE FIRST PART of Wanda's idea I did not think was great. I thought the first part of her idea smelled as bad as the mitt we were looking for. Willie thought the same, too.

But McGurk and Wanda made us go through with it. It was this.

We had to dress up.

McGurk and Willie and me, we had to dress up.

*In women's hats!*

No kidding.

Wanda borrowed two out of her mother's sewing room, and McGurk borrowed one from his. All of them those great big floppy things with broad brims and ribbons.

You think that was bad enough?

Wait. There was more. : . .

We also had to wear some women's frilly shirts that Wanda dug out from some junk box at home.

"Oh, no!" said Willie, when she tossed them onto the table in the McGurk Organization Headquarters. "The hat I don't mind, because its brim is so big it will hide my face. But those things—no."

"Me neither," I said.

"Am *I* beefing?" said McGurk. "No. I am not. In this business you wear anything if it helps solve a mystery."

"They won't look so bad with the swords and

belts," said Wanda.

Well, maybe they wouldn't have, at that. If there'd been real swords and real sword belts. But the belts she had in mind were just ordinary old belts and the swords were just sticks that had been covered with silver paint.

"There you are," she said, when we'd gotten everything on. "The Three Musketeers."

"Who *were* those three guys anyhow?" said Willie.

"The finest swordsmen in the whole of France," said Wanda. "You ought to be proud."

"Yeah, well," said Willie, waving his stick around and trying to look fierce. "If it wasn't for these ribbons. . . ."

"Ribbons or no ribbons," I said, "swords or no swords, you don't get *me* going out of here dressed like *this*."

Then McGurk thought of the beards.

"Hold it!" he said, and went dashing out of the room.

Inside two minutes he was back with an old Movie Make-Up Kit he once got for Christmas.

"Help yourself to some whiskers, fellers," he said.

"Now you're talking!" said Willie, fixing himself up with a pair of long, black Chinese mustaches.

"You bet!" I said, slipping on one of those little pointed Devil beards.

"O.K., so let's go!" said McGurk, through a great, bushy red Old Timer beard.

And with a wave of his sword he led us out.

Now I have to be fair to Wanda. It certainly was a good idea once we'd gotten over our shyness. I mean it certainly worked.

Mrs. Lorrimore couldn't have been more cooperative.

"Hello, what's this?" she said, when she came to the door. "Trick or Treat in the middle of *August?*"

"No, no!" said Wanda, waving toward us. "Just dressing up. Meet the Three Musketeers!"

Then McGurk gave Willie a shove, and Willie stepped forward the way we'd planned it.

"My sword is. . . ."

For a second I thought he was going to forget his line. Then he went on:

"My sword is at your command, ma'am!"

Again I thought he was going to forget, but McGurk muttered something through his red bush and he gave Willie another shove which took him right up close to Mrs. Lorrimore.

Then Willie swept off his hat and did a deep bow, and McGurk and I, we did the same, only Willie did something else. He did what the whole thing had been leading up to. He grabbed Mrs. Lorrimore's left hand and kissed it.

"M-m-m-munch!" he went.

She was tickled pink. Not just by his mustaches. I mean she was tickled by the whole performance.

"How cute!" she said.

With Mrs. Gallo it worked also, when we visited her.

"Hey! What you doing?" she yelled, when Willie grabbed her hand. (She's the nervous type.)

But she too was tickled when Willie kissed it.

"Now I call that real sweet!" she said. "Come again when I'm not on the phone."

Mrs. Henshaw went one better than both the other ladies. Mrs. Henshaw is the dreamy type and she really loved the treatment. What made it specially good was that Willie and McGurk and me were getting the feel of the thing by then, and we were beginning to enjoy it, so we were doing some really fancy bowing and hat-sweeping.

So Mrs. Henshaw didn't simply say how cute or how sweet, when Willie kissed her hand. No, sir. She closed her eyes, she gave a big sigh, then she smiled all over her face and said:

"On shanty, Miss Sewer."

That's French. In American it doesn't seem to make sense, but in French it means:

"I am enchanted by you, sir!"

I know this because I asked her, and I got her to write it down in my notebook, and here it is, showing you the real French spelling:

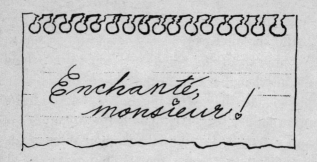

*Enchanté, monsieur!*

"Look at the way she puts little hearts instead of points," I said, on the way back.

"That's just like *her*," said Wanda.

"When I grow up I might decide to be an actor after all," said Willie, looking very proud.

"Quit the yacking!" snarled McGurk. "We have a lot of hard thinking to do."

Well, he was right.

Because—cute, sweet, or *enchanté*—Wanda's plan hadn't gotten us much further. None of those women's hands had given off a single little whiff of the missing mitt. Neither had Mrs. Grieg's when Wanda had checked her out earlier.

So we were back to where we'd started, and

when we looked at it that way it made us feel less pleased with our performance. All we felt then was that we'd looked like fools, wearing these sissy clothes, and it had gotten us exactly nowhere.

"Will we *ever* solve this mystery?" I was beginning to wonder, as we crossed the Mc-Gurk lawn. "Will we *ever* be able to save Willie from being taken off his aunt's Handsome Gift List for the rest of his life?"

Whatever doubts I had about his nose, I'd grown to like this thin, sad guy who'd come to live among us. And I want you to know that it was for his sake as much as the Organization's that I was feeling so miserable, crossing that yard. Already I had torn off the floppy hat and the frilly shirt. Then I threw the pointed black Devil beard at Wanda's back to see if it would stick there and make *her* look a fool, but it missed. So I had to pick it up, and I tripped over my sword, and I began to wonder if anything would ever go right for us again, mystery or no mystery.

And you know what?

That's exactly when things *did* start to work out for us.

I didn't know it at the time.

All I knew at the time was that we seemed to have touched bottom.

But, as I lay sprawled out on the grass, up rushed Sammy, the Henshaw dog, laughing all over his face, and he made a dive at the floppy hat I'd dropped, and I only just managed to grab it back before he could latch onto it.

"Oh no, you don't!" I said.

And even though I didn't know it *then*, that's where our luck started to turn.

# CHAPTER SEVEN

## *The Suspect*

THE BASEMENT HEADQUARTERS of the McGurk
Organization was beginning to look real businesslike.

The files were still pretty bare, sure. The one
marked LATEST MYSTERY, RECORDS AND CLUES
was full of shadows. The DETAILS OF SUSPECTS
had in it only the page from my notebook with

the Welcome Wagon list. (And all *those* names were now crossed out.) As for the MYSTERIES SOLVED box, it contained just one thing: a tiny red spider.

But the files were stacked neatly enough, side by side at one end of the table. I mean they looked businesslike enough to anyone who didn't bother to peep inside. And so did my typewriter in the middle of the table, with its cover off, all ready to type down evidence and records and things. Even Willie's pack of paper, next to the typewriter, looked business-like—with the first clean pages jutting out at the top, ready to be plucked out and typed on.

But what looked even more businesslike than all this was the wall behind the table. McGurk had been busy taping things to it. The biggest of these things, slap in the middle, was a street map of the whole of our city, which he'd borrowed from his Dad's den. And in the middle of this street map, in the middle of our street, he had pinned this old red button. It was one of those campaign button things and it said on it:

**"THIS IS WHERE IT'S AT BABY!"**

Now the IT could have meant anything, I guess, depending on where you wore it. McGurk said it was supposed to be pinned just over the heart. But what the IT meant now was Willie's house: the Scene of the Crime. And that brings me to the second thing taped on the wall, which you had better study carefully, because it is important.

Tied to the button was a piece of red string. This piece of string was stretched out to the side of the street map, and the other end of it was taped to this second thing. This second thing was the floor plan of Willie's house. It was headed:

THE SCENE OF THE CRIME

and this is a copy of it:

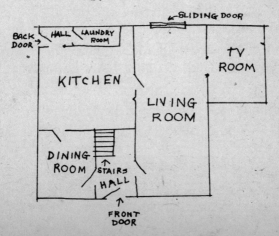

McGurk was real proud of that plan. He was a bit miffed when I pointed out that it didn't show any windows, but I have to be fair and admit that it didn't really matter. That plan turned out to be useful enough without showing windows, believe me!

Anyway, as I said, it all looked very businesslike in the basement headquarters of the McGurk Organization that morning. It was only the *officers* of the Organization that didn't look businesslike.

They looked weary. Puzzled. Licked.

Willie picked out the Welcome Wagon list from the file. He looked at it as if it smelled worse than any catcher's mitt could. Then he dropped it back in.

"They're clean," he said. "All clean."

McGurk just grunted. He was standing in front of the Scene of the Crime plan. He was looking at it as if it didn't smell any too good either.

Wanda was folding up the frilly shirts. She was looking as if she was wondering if it had been worth it after all, joining the Organization. She had a kind of sad look in her eyes, as if she was hankering for the top of her tree.

And me, I was looking at Willie's typewriter paper and wondering if I'd ever get to use it.

Then McGurk called Willie over to his side.

"Let's just go over this again," he said, tapping the plan with a pencil. "You say everyone went into the living room when the Welcome Wagon came."

"Yes!" said Willie wearily. "How many more times?"

Then Wanda looked up from the shirts.

"Oh no, they didn't!"

"Huh?" said McGurk.

"No," said Wanda, coming across to the plan.

"Well, *I* don't remember anyone not going in there," said Willie, looking down his nose at her.

"No," said Wanda. "Because *you're* the one who didn't go into the living room. *You* stayed out. In the front hall. Sulking."

Willie slapped his forehead.

"Oh, yes! Sure! But I wasn't sulking." He turned to McGurk. "I was standing by the front door wondering if any of you guys were gonna come to welcome *me*. I mean, at least to stop by and say hello."

"We leave that kind of thing to the women-folks," said McGurk. "But never mind that now. This is interesting. It means that nobody could have sneaked in by the front door if you were there. Right?"

"Right," said Willie. "But—"

"And nobody could have come in through the sliding door at the back," said Wanda. "Because that's in the living room and *we* would have seen them."

"Fine!" said McGurk. "Now we're getting somewhere. It means that whoever did it must have come in at the back door, here."

He tapped the place.

But Willie was shaking his head.

"No. Sorry."

"But they *must* have!"

"Nuh-huh! They *couldn't* have," said Willie.

"On account it was locked. We didn't find the key till late last night. It was a nuisance. It meant the moving men had to carry all the kitchen stuff in at the front."

"Oh."

Suddenly we all stopped looking business-like again.

Willie sighed.

"Anyway," he said, "whoever stole the mitt would have to get upstairs, wouldn't they? So even if they could have snuck in at the back, they'd still have to get past me in the front hall."

Then it was McGurk who sighed.

He went and flopped down on his rocking chair.

"I don't suppose you could pick up the trail, Willie?" he said. "I mean with your nose to the ground?"

This made Willie mad.

"Whaddya think I *am?*" he said. "A dog? You're darned right I couldn't. My nose isn't *that* sensitive!"

Then I jumped.

It must have been the word "dog" that did it. That and the memory of what had just happened to me out in the McGurk yard.

"Just a minute!" I said, feeling suddenly excited. "How about if a *dog* came in, Willie? Would you have thought to put that on your list?"

Willie frowned. Then he looked at Wanda. "Hey, come to think of it, a dog did come in."

"I didn't see any dog," said Wanda.

"But you must have," said Willie. "It came tagging along behind the rest of you. I thought it belonged to one of the ladies."

"Yes, but did you actually see it go into the living room?" I asked. "I mean could it have gone wandering off up the stairs behind your back?"

"Well, I guess so. But—"

"Aha!" roared McGurk, swinging right out of his chair. "Now listen carefully, Willie. It wouldn't have been a beagle, would it? Male, black ears, brown head, white patches?"

"Yeah," said Willie. "Something like that. In fact, it was out in your yard just now, tangling with Joey here—"

"*Sammy!*" cried McGurk and Wanda and me, all together. "Sammy Henshaw!"

And we looked at one another, wondering why we hadn't thought of him before.

Even Willie looked as if he could have kicked himself, and he didn't even know that dog and his thieving ways.

But Willie had another reason for looking that way.

"Why, sure!" he said. "That accounts for it!"

"Accounts for what?" said McGurk, now raring to go.

"The mark," said Willie.

"What mark?"

"On the paper pack that was on top of the crate. This one."

He went to the table and picked up the pack. He turned it over, put his face closer and pointed.

"Yes. Look. This smudge here."

We all stared at the smudge.

It was very very faint, but that smudge and the piece of wrapping paper it was on is now Exhibit Number One in the Case of the Missing Mitt. Here it is:

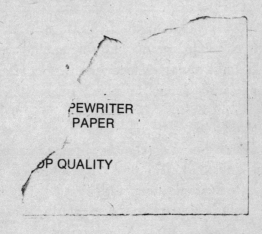

PEWRITER
PAPER

P QUALITY

"A dog's paw mark!" said McGurk.

"That part of the paper seems to have been wet," said Wanda. "Kind of smeared."

"Yes," I said. "I bet it's where Sammy drooled when he found the mitt."

We looked at one another again. Even Mc-

Gurk had gone a bit red. I mean we'd had this clue all along. On our table. In our headquarters. And we hadn't even noticed it!

"I thought it was just a rat's print," said Willie. "Or—or something. You know. From the warehouse."

"A *rat?*" cried McGurk. "*This* size?"

But he didn't go on with the bawling out he looked like giving Officer Sandowsky. After all, he was just as much to blame for not noticing it himself. Besides, McGurk isn't one for looking back.

"Men," he said, slapping down the paper pack and staring around, "I think we're very close to making an arrest!"

"Yeah!" said Willie. "And getting my mitt back. What are we waiting for?"

For once he looked like beating McGurk to the door.

But:

"Hold it," said McGurk. "Just another couple of minutes. This has got to be done in style,

82

and as Head of the Organization I have to prepare for it."

# CHAPTER EIGHT

## *The Search*

I BET YOU can't guess what McGurk's idea was.
I mean his idea of preparing for an arrest.

I bet if I gave you a million tries you would
never get it.

So I'll tell you.

That guy's idea of making an arrest in style
was to go upstairs and put on his best suit.

No kidding.

As his Mom said afterwards:

"If *I* ask you to put on your best suit for something *regular*, it is different. If *I* ask you to put it on for visiting with your Grandmother McGurk, or for church, or for anything like that, it is murder. You say you will be too hot. Or feel too tied up. One time you told me it made you have a rash. But for *this*, no. For this you can put on your best suit."

Mind you, his Mom had good reason to bawl him out afterwards. I mean it wasn't just ordinary Mom-talk. But we'll get to that later.

Right now, we were on our way to the Henshaw's place. Willie and Wanda and I were dressed in our ordinary clothes, but McGurk—well—he looked incredible. He had put on his *very* best suit. Blue, light blue. And a shirt with a collar. And one of his father's silk neckties. And some shiny black shoes.

You could tell just by looking at him that he was all set to celebrate. Not just the solving of the mystery. Not just putting Willie in the clear with his aunt, either. Oh, no. McGurk was all set to celebrate the ten-dollar bill we now looked like getting, and all the fingerprint powder and stuff it would buy.

Naturally, he was the one who rang the Henshaw doorbell. And when Mrs. Henshaw came and saw him looking so sharp, she started looking enchanted again.

"Hi!" she said. "To what do I owe this great honor?"

But she didn't look quite so enchanted when he flashed his I.D. card and said:

"I'm afraid we've come on official business, ma'am."

"Oh, gosh!" said Mrs. Henshaw. "I didn't know anyone had seen me double-park outside the library, officer."

"It's not that, ma'am," said Wanda. "It isn't anything *you've* done."

The lady brightened up.

"Ah, I think I know, then!" she said. "You've come making inquiries about three wild Frenchmen, haven't you? Did they escape from somewhere?"

"This is no joke, ma'am," said McGurk. "This is a real crime."

"Yeah!" said Willie. "My brand-new catcher's mitt. It was stolen yesterday."

"And we have reason to believe," I said, wanting to take part myself, "that—"

But McGurk shushed me and went on with it himself.

"We have reason to believe that your dog— uh—Samuel Henshaw—is involved in the case."

Mrs. Henshaw rolled her eyes and groaned.

"Oh, not *again!* He's not started *that* again, has he?"

"Did you notice him with such an article?" said McGurk. "Did you notice him bring anything into the house, yesterday morning?"

"No," said Mrs. Henshaw. "Nor would I be likely to. You see, he stopped bringing things *into* the house months ago. When he realized we would take them off him. Now he only takes things *out*."

"Yes, and out of other people's houses, too!" said Wanda.

"Oh, and he used to be *such* a good dog!"

said Mrs. Henshaw. "For a beagle, anyway. Oh, what will he do next? Oh, my baby!"

"Disgusting!" muttered Wanda, behind me. She doesn't think much of Mrs. Henshaw, I guess.

"Just calm down, ma'am," said McGurk. "It's not your fault."

"The heck it's not!" muttered Wanda. "If people go and spoil their dogs, how can you—?"

But McGurk gave her a stern look and shushed her, too.

"Anyway, ma'am," he said, "the sooner we recover the property, the better. Mind if we take a look around?"

"But it won't be in the house!" moaned Mrs. Henshaw. "I tell you—"

"No. We realize that. But maybe if we looked around in the yard?"

Mrs. Henshaw waved us on.

"Why, sure," she said. "Do. Please. Go ahead. I'll give you all the help I can. Maybe it's in his kennel around the back."

McGurk thanked her. He was still very

polite, but he told us after that if she hadn't given us permission he would have sent me right back to headquarters to type out a Search Warrant.

Then the phone rang and she had to go in.

"Right. Let's get onto it, men!" said McGurk.

And he led the way around the back to the kennel.

Kennel?

Some kennel!

More like a doll's house.

It was the regular kennel shape. Maybe a bit big and deep for a dog like Sammy. But after that there was no likeness to any dog kennel *I* ever saw.

It was painted bright brick red, for a start. And on the bright brick red they'd painted little windows. No kidding. With all the trimmings, like little white crisscross window frames and fancy curtains and window boxes and things. And the roof—you just have to believe this—it was like on a gingerbread house in a fairy tale. Very steep, with birds and things carved out of the overhanging bits, and a little weathervane on top. Truly! Shaped like a cat and painted gold.

But best of all was the front, all around the door. Painted roses! And a sign: CHEZ SAM— which is more French and means THE HOUSE OF SAM.

And that's all about the kennel, because right now, at that door, with the roses all around him and a big grin on his face, out came Sammy.

Just his head at first.

The rest of him stayed inside, where we could hear his tail thumping the floor.

"I bet," said McGurk, "he's got the mitt in there."

"Right!" said Willie, sticking out his arm. "This is where—"

"Grrr!" went Sammy.

Willie's hand stopped dead. It was his left hand.

It was as if he'd remembered that the finest catcher's mitts in the world are no good to a guy without a left hand.

He wasn't for trying his right, either.

"Good dog!" said McGurk.

"Grrr!" went Sammy.

He was still grinning. His tail was still thumping away. But those teeth sure looked sharp.

"Oh, come out of the way!" said Wanda, pushing past us. "That dog's too silly to do you any harm!"

And without stopping, she shot out her hand, grabbed Sammy by the collar, and hoiked him clean out.

"Be careful with him," said McGurk. "We haven't *proved* he's the thief. We don't want anyone accusing us of police brutality!"

"He's enjoying it!" said Wanda. "Go on! Stand back!" she said to the dog, clapping her hands on her knees. This sent Sammy dancing around behind us, barking with joy.

Or was it joy?

Was it maybe *rage*, at the sight of McGurk groping around inside of his kennel?

"Keep him back," grunted McGurk. "There's all sorts of—huh!—what's this?"

He handed out a rubber duck, with its head missing.

"That's little Tony Gallo's!" cried Wanda.

"And this?" grunted McGurk, heaving out a woman's shoe. "And this?—and this?—"

So the stuff kept coming out, with Sammy

nearly going wild, and Wanda getting all indignant, and Willie getting impatient, and me —well—just being observant, knowing I would have to write down all the things in my report.

And these other things were:

> a pearl-backed hairbrush with most of the
> bristles missing;
> a tobacco pouch;
> a wooden ball; and
> one of those things like a saddle with three
> holes in the corners and a cow's head
> stamped on it, which they use to make
> the seats of fishing stools out of.

"And that," grunted McGurk, groping around and making empty noises in the kennel, so that Willie got to look very sad indeed, "that looks like it. . . . Huh! No. Wait. . . ." He pulled something out. "Hey! D'you think *this* could be—?"

"Gosh!"

"Yeah!"

We all gasped as we crowded around.

There was no mistaking the smell, even in that condition.

But the *shape!*

It didn't look like a catcher's mitt any more. I didn't look like anything much except an old chewed-up piece of leather. Or one of those pellets that owls cough up. You know. When they eat a whole mouse and cough up just its skin and maybe a bone or two.

And—just as the pellet that an owl coughs up is always smaller than the animal or bird that was the meal in the first place—so the catcher's mitt seemed to have shrunk too.

"He must have chewed it like it was gum!" said McGurk, looking real awed.

"You're a bad dog!" said Wanda.

Sammy just grinned from a safe distance up the yard, with his tongue out.

And Willie—poor Willie—he looked ready to cry.

By now I had taken the thing from McGurk and I was busy inspecting it myself.

Why I was doing this I don't know, except

that I knew this was something else I would have to describe.

And then, as I unpicked that shapeless thing that still reeked of leather, I found a very interesting clue.

"Well, at least he didn't eat the label," I said. "Look."

Willie nearly went mad.

"Label?" he cried. "Label-schmabel! What good is a label to me now? What good will it do to show Aunt Mabel a lousy stinking label?"

This sounded just like poetry, sure. But there wasn't time to enjoy it. There wasn't time to tell Willie that in his agony he was talking just like Shakespeare.

Right now I was busy unscrewing that tag of cloth. And when I'd done that, and spread it out, and put it the right way up, I cried out myself.

"Hey! Read this!"

Here is that label, which is now Exhibit Number Two in our file on the Mystery of the Missing Mitt:

```
❖❖❖❖❖❖❖❖❖❖❖❖❖❖❖❖❖❖❖❖❖❖❖
        AUTOGLOVES
             ♣
          Size 9½
      BEST IMLEATHER ®
❖❖❖❖❖❖❖❖❖❖❖❖❖❖❖❖❖❖❖❖❖❖❖
```

"What's Imleather?" said Wanda.

"Imitation leather, I guess," said McGurk.

"We *know* that!" howled Willie. "And what are *you* grinning at, fella? What's so funny?"

He was looking at me, and he was madder than ever.

And, sure enough, I *was* grinning. But not because I thought it was funny.

No, sir.

"Forget the Imleather bit," I said. "How about *this?* The Autogloves bit?"

"Well?" said McGurk—and I'd like you to note this—even he was puzzled.

"Well!" I said. "This isn't the remains of Willie's catcher's mitt at all! This is the remains of one of my Dad's driving gloves. Sammy must have dug it up!"

Everybody crowded closer.

Then McGurk said:

"Well, I wonder where—"

Which is the exact moment that Sammy woofed.

That woof had everything in it.

Smartness.

Jeering.

Triumph.

And a challenge.

We all looked around.

"Hey!" cried Willie. "Lookit! My mitt!"

When he said, "Hey!" the mitt was on the grass in front of Sammy's jeering nose.

When he said, "Lookit!" the mitt was in Sammy's triumphant mouth.

And when he said, "My mitt!" all we could see of Sammy was his challenging tail as he went tearing off across the yards.

# CHAPTER NINE

## *The Chase*

WHERE SAMMY HAD had the mitt stashed we never did find out. Maybe in the garage. Maybe in some extra-special hiding place under some bushes. Maybe somewhere in that yard he had an even bigger collection of loot than in his kennel.

But we were only interested in the mitt just

then. We were only interested in getting it back in one piece. We were only interested in getting it before he'd had time to do with it what he'd done to that driving glove.

So the chase around the back yards began.

At first there was a lot of yelling.

McGurk kept shouting police-type things like:

"Freeze!" and

"Hold it!" and

"Drop it, you hear?"

Wanda tried to be more coaxing. She kept shouting:

"Good dog. That's a good dog. Here, Sammy-boy!"

And Willie's cries were different again. He was so upset—so glad to have traced that mitt, so mad to see it take off again so fast—that I guess he didn't know what he was yelling. *He* kept calling the dog bad names. So Mrs. Gallo got into the act and yelled too. Except that *she* yelled after Willie:

"Young man, is that the way they talk in

Cleveland? You wash that mouth out!"

As for me, I saved my breath. The way I figured it was this:

Even if Sammy could understand, he must have been getting all mixed up. I mean with McGurk yelling at him to Hold It one minute and Drop It the next. And with Wanda praising him and Willie cussing him.

Besides, I could see we should need all our breath for running and jumping and swerving and diving. The way that dog was going I could tell we had a long chase ahead of us. I knew about beagles. Any dog that is bred to hunt hares and rabbits must be fast. And, believe me, that Sammy could GO.

Then again, the territory suited him. All those back yards. All those places for a dog to sneak in and hide and take a breather before laughing at you again, picking up the mitt, and showing you his waving tail.

In our neighborhood there aren't many fences between the yards.

But there are other obstacles, of course.

Like bushes. And old junk lying around. And places thick with weeds like a jungle. And flower beds and vegetable patches. And one or two of those things they call compost heaps.

Well, mostly *they* worked in Sammy's favor, too.

He *used* the bushes. He had us going around and in and out the Pabsts' blueberries until we were dizzy and falling over one another. And when we thought we'd cornered him under the Winstons' holly bush, all we got were scratches up our arms.

In the jungle patches, that dog seemed to know where all the poison ivy was and where the yellow jackets and other biting bugs were. Of course, they didn't trouble him, but Wanda still has a rash on her arm from the ivy, and McGurk and Willie and me all got stung or bitten. In fact, if Sammy had had the sense to stay in those places, maybe we never would have caught up with him.

But no. That dog liked to live dangerously. So when he heard from our yells and groans how we'd been suffering in there, he lit out for the cultivated places. Yet even that didn't seem to help us at first.

I mean *he* could go on taking short cuts across people's beautiful flower beds while we had to go all the way around. And *he* could go charging through old Gramp Martin's vegetable patch and get away with it, while we knew it would be more than our hides were worth.

Still and all, it was in Gramp Martin's yard that at last it looked like he was trapped, so I guess we couldn't really complain.

I mentioned before about compost heaps, didn't I?

Well, there was one in Gramp Martin's yard. In the corner between the end of his garage and the shed he keeps his gardening tools in. And if you don't know what a compost heap is, it is what organic gardeners have: heaps of rotten stuff to put on their soil to make it rich. Me, I call them garbage heaps, because that's what they are, really. Old rotten vegetables and things. Rotten old fruit and stuff from the kitchen and dead leaves. Sometimes horse or cow manure. And the smell—wow! How Willie, with *his* sensitive nose, ever went near that heap of old man Martin's and *lived*, I shall never know.

Anyway, that's where Sammy had ended up, after he'd had us dodging around the vegetables. Straight up the long, sloping, stinking heap in that corner.

McGurk could hardly believe his luck.

"Right, men, we have him now. He's cornered. Fan out a little so he can't slip by. Then leave the rest to me."

Well, he was boss. If *he* wanted to go slowly stalking that dog right into the farthest corner of *that* mess, it was O.K. by me. Right enough, I didn't have *my* best suit on, but if that was the way McGurk wanted it, O.K., O.K.

The others must have thought the same. Even Willie, eager as he was to get that mitt back. All at once he looked as if he'd decided there were worse things in life than getting crossed off his aunt's Handsome Gift List.

Probably he *was* suffering from the smell, at that, with his extra-sensitive nose and all.

So it was left to the Boss Man. The Head of the Organization.

And right away, just by looking at the gleam in McGurk's eyes, I could tell what was running through *his* mind. The click of Aunt Mabel's purse and the rustle of a crisp new ten-dollar bill. That's what. The click could be the purse opening or it could be the purse closing. The rustle could be the bill going into Willie's hand or it could be the bill going back into Aunt Mabel's purse. It all depended on McGurk.

"O.K." he said to the dog, which had found a dry patch right at the top in the corner—an old loaf or something—to rest on. "Give me that mitt, Sammy,"

Sammy shook his head, with the mitt in his mouth, and McGurk took a step forward.

*Squelch!*

That was the shine gone off one shoe.

"Come on, now. We've got you cornered."

Another shake, another step, another squelch.

McGurk was up to his ankles.

But his arm was out and we could tell, and he could tell, that another two inches and he'd be touching the mitt.

Sammy could tell, too. He crouched very still.

"O.K.!" growled McGurk. "You asked for this!"

And he made one quick grab that took his hand forward that extra two inches.

In fact, it was so quick and so eager that it took him forward much more than those two inches. It took him forward at least ten. And not just the hand. It took the head forward too, and the shoulders, and the chest, and the whole body. Because what happened was he slipped, he was so eager to close the case, and —with his lovely blue suit, and his shirt with a collar, and his father's silk necktie—he went slap into that goo.

The rest of us were so startled we just stood

there, not daring to laugh, of course, but also not knowing whether to help him up or spare his feelings by pretending nothing had happened. You know how it is. And while we were standing like that, off between us slithered Sammy, the mitt still in his mouth.

Boy, what a chase that was!

By now other kids and dogs were joining in. Mrs. Prochick thought there was a riot and nearly called the police. Everybody was yelling, with McGurk—game to the end—leading the pack and sounding as mad as Willie now.

Then we reached the Sandowskys' yard. The old boxes and containers and cartons were still in a heap.

Now I mentioned earlier about piles of junk being obstacles. Well, so far they'd all been in Sammy's favor.

Not this time, though.

No, sir.

Because you know what that dumb dog did?

He headed straight for that heap, and into the center of it, and right into the mouth of that big wooden box that Willie had stood on his head to get into, and which he'd left lying on its side.

This time we made no mistake.

We all stood side by side, legs together, at attention, an inch in front of that box, so that there was no way for Sammy to escape. Then McGurk reached in with a hand and arm and sleeve that were still slimy from the compost heap, and he said:

"*Give!*"

And Sammy gave.

Only one thing was worrying Willie now. With his face all anxious, he peered at the mitt.

"Gee!" he said. "I hope—"

But it was O.K. The inscription wasn't all that badly damaged.

"We can ink in the chewed-off letters so she'll never notice," he said, pointing to the message:

*HAPPY CAT ING!*

*YOUR OVING AUNT ABEL.*

And that was that. I mean apart from Mrs. McGurk giving McGurk a Grade One bawling-out on account of the suit.

But that didn't worry *him*.

Why should it?

The McGurk Organization had solved its very first mystery.

"Why," he said, "we can now add to the notice on the door."

So he got out the marking pen and under the words PRIVATE INVESTIGATIONS and MYSTERIES SOLVED he added:

100 per cent SUCCESS RECORD

Then, maybe because it had been a catcher's mitt that had started it all, he changed his mind, crossed those words out, and put instead:

BATTING AVERAGE - 1.000

## The Chase

Oh, yes. And one thing more.

We didn't get the ten dollars after all. Not exactly. You see, when Willie's Aunt Mabel came to spend the weekend, McGurk said:

"Listen. Let's show her some action. Let's show her how well you can use the mitt. Then maybe she'll make it *fifteen* dollars for your new hobby."

Well, maybe she would have, at that. If McGurk hadn't put too much beef into one of his throws. And if Willie hadn't been smiling *gratefully* at Aunt Mabel (the way McGurk had been coaching him to) instead of watching what he was doing. And if the ball hadn't curved way past his mitt and through the kitchen window (closed).

So although Willie got the ten dollars in the end, five of them had to go toward repairing the damage. Personally, I thought it should have come out of McGurk's allowance. He was the guy who *threw* the ball. That's usually who pays.

But McGurk wouldn't go for that. It had happened in the course of business, he said. Fund raising.

"So charge it to business expenses," he said. So we did.

E. W. HILDICK has written more than thirty books for children, published both here and in his native England. Among his outstanding books published here are *The Dragon That Lived Under Manhattan, Manhattan Is Missing, The Secret Winners, Top Boy At Twisters Creek, Louie's S.O.S.,* and *Louie's Lot,* which won the Hans Christian Andersen Award Diploma of Honor for 1968.

A former teacher, E. W. Hildick and his wife divide their time between their house in England and the United States.